The Cricket and the Frog
I0606692
Written By:
Donald C Robertson Sr. M. Ed. B.A.

Bound and printed in St. Charles Missouri

Acknowledgement

Writing this book has been a fulfilling and transformative journey, and I am deeply grateful to the many individuals who have played a significant role in making it possible.

Their support, guidance, and encouragement have been invaluable, and I would like to extend my heartfelt acknowledgments to the following:

My Family: To my family, the foundation of my strength and inspiration. Thank you for standing by me, understanding the demands of the creative process, and offering unwavering support. Your belief in me and your love have been my guiding lights throughout this endeavor.

The Readers: I extend my deepest gratitude to all the readers who will embark on this literary adventure. Your curiosity and openness to explore new narratives make the world of literature a wondrous place. It is my sincerest hope that my stories touch your hearts and leave a positive impact on your lives.

With a heart full of gratitude and appreciation, I thank each and every one of you for being a part of this book's creation and for supporting me as an author.

Sincerely,

Dedication

To my family, friends, and readers—your support and encouragement mean the world to me. It is my pleasure to bring to you stories that inspire, excite, and challenge your imagination. If I can help one child through my writing, I will have achieved my dream.

In closing, I extend my great appreciation to everyone who has been a part of this journey. Your love, support, and enthusiasm have made this book a reality. It is my sincere hope that the stories held within these pages will inspire, entertain, and bring joy to your hearts.

With love and appreciation,

Donald C Robertson Sr

Once upon a time, a cricket named Dana lived in a peaceful magical forest. He gained a reputation for the beautiful music he made playing his violin and melodious chirping. Dana played solo performances every night for anyone who would listen.

The other animals in the forest loved listening to Dana's music. His solo performances were like attending a concert given by a well accomplished artist.

However, the loud unscripted sounds of the other animals living in the forest often drowned out his music or forced him to stop playing all together.

GROOOOHP!
OORP!

One night, as Dana was playing
his music he heard a strange
sound coming from the
nearby pond.

It was rhythmic and harmonic,
and led by a musical frog name
Marvin. He and his frog choir
were practicing and making
beautiful musical sounds.

Dana introduces himself and said, "Hi I am Dana, I am a musician and I play the violin. I could not help but hear you and your choir's singing.

Marvin then introduced himself and his choir, and mentioned that they sang there each night hoping to draw some fans, hopefully some girls.

Marvin explained that he always only wanted to be more than the leader of a small frog choir, but always dreamed of becoming a conductor of a large choir and orchestra.

He thought that by combining various sounds from the animals in the forest, he could create a musical symphony.

Dana was thrilled to find Marvin, as he felt that his violin would be an excellent addition to the small choir of musical frogs.

Dana agreed to perform with the frogs, he could see that Marvin was an excellent con-ductor and made Dana feel welcomed. Together they worked tirelessly practicing night after night.

After hearing the beautiful music the other animals be-gan to investigate to see how they could be a part of this new group.

The first to stop by was Simon the owl, he inquired, WHO, WHO, WHO is making that wonderful music. I am Simon the owl and I love the music that you were making and wanted to add my hooting sound to the musical mixture. Simon said that he often made that hooting sound when was trying to attract a mate. Marvin was excited to hear Simon's voice and explained that he would love to have Simon join to choir.

They were stopped by a loud screeching sound and the flutter of wings. Hanging down from a branch over the group, were two large bats, Freddy and Chris.

Freddy said, "We screech and flutter to vocalize with other bats."

They landed next to Marvin and said, "We would love to join the group and could contribute to the choir. Dana agreed and said, "Please join us"

The next animal to come to the group was Ricky the Raccoon. Ricky had a wide range of sounds which included: giggling, hissing, chirping, and snarling, that he used as he searched for food and water during the dark hours of the night. Dana thought Ricky would also work well with the group and invited him to join right up.

Arline was a nightjar, she and the other nightjars had a distinctive melody and repetitive note churring and trilling as they communicated.

 What a wonderful sound Dana said, "We need those sounds in our tenor section. Please join us." Arline and her friends agreed.

Finally, Steven the friendly skunk stopped by and asked if he could join the choir. Steven who had a very low sounding hiss and rustling sound he made as he walked through the forest. He was very proper and quite pleas-ant. However, we were very aware not to annoyed Steven due to the very smelly spray that he could emit.

Other animals came to add their voices, but one very special animal was Evon the red tail Fox. She was well known in the forest for her silky sexy bark and high-pitched screams. When she gave out her scream and raised her tail it signaled that there was no more danger. Marvin was impressed that Evon wanted to join his choir and Marvin quickly agreed.

All of the animals Dana had select-
ed arrived at practice and began to
sing and play their instruments.
Marvin gave instructions to each
member as to how he wanted
them to add their sounds and music. Crowds gathered as they prac-
ticed and the other animals loved
the musical orchestra and they all
cheered. Yay!!!   Yay!!

As the Orchestra/Choir grew in size, it became necessary to find a large enough place for them to practice and perform. Dana chose an area next to a larger pond.

Marvin's small choir had now become an orchestra of many sounds and could produce wonderful music.

Marvin suddenly realized that his small group of animals had grown and he was now the leader of an orchestra.

Each with their own distinctive sounds and voices. He assigned each person their part, and would point at them when he was ready for them to join in.

Marvin started by pointing to Dana the Cricket and he began with his beautiful string solo: he then pointed to the frogs who joined with their low bass croak, croak croak: Next he pointed to Simon the Owl and he added in a soft repetitive Hoot, Hoot, HOOT HOOOOO.

Next he pointed to Jeff and Chris the bats, to flutter then screech, next Rick the Raccoon added his hissing and growling sound followed by his giggling. As the music grew louder he pointed to Arline and her friends to make her trilling sound as loud as they could, and Steven added his quiet rustling then loud barking sound, and finally he pointed at Evon to let out her loud scream then raise her tail to end the music.

Everyone was very pleased with how they had come to-gether to make the beautiful song of the forest. Now Marvin was ready for the live performance to see if the other animals would enjoy it as much as he did.

However, little did they know they weren't the only ones pleased with the little orchestra's achievement. In fact there was one animal looking for more than a musical performance, but a Meal!!! Willie the Coyote, he was a mean scary predator that was feared by all of the animals of the forest. He had been watching them and, began planning his own contribution to the orchestra and it would not be pleasant.

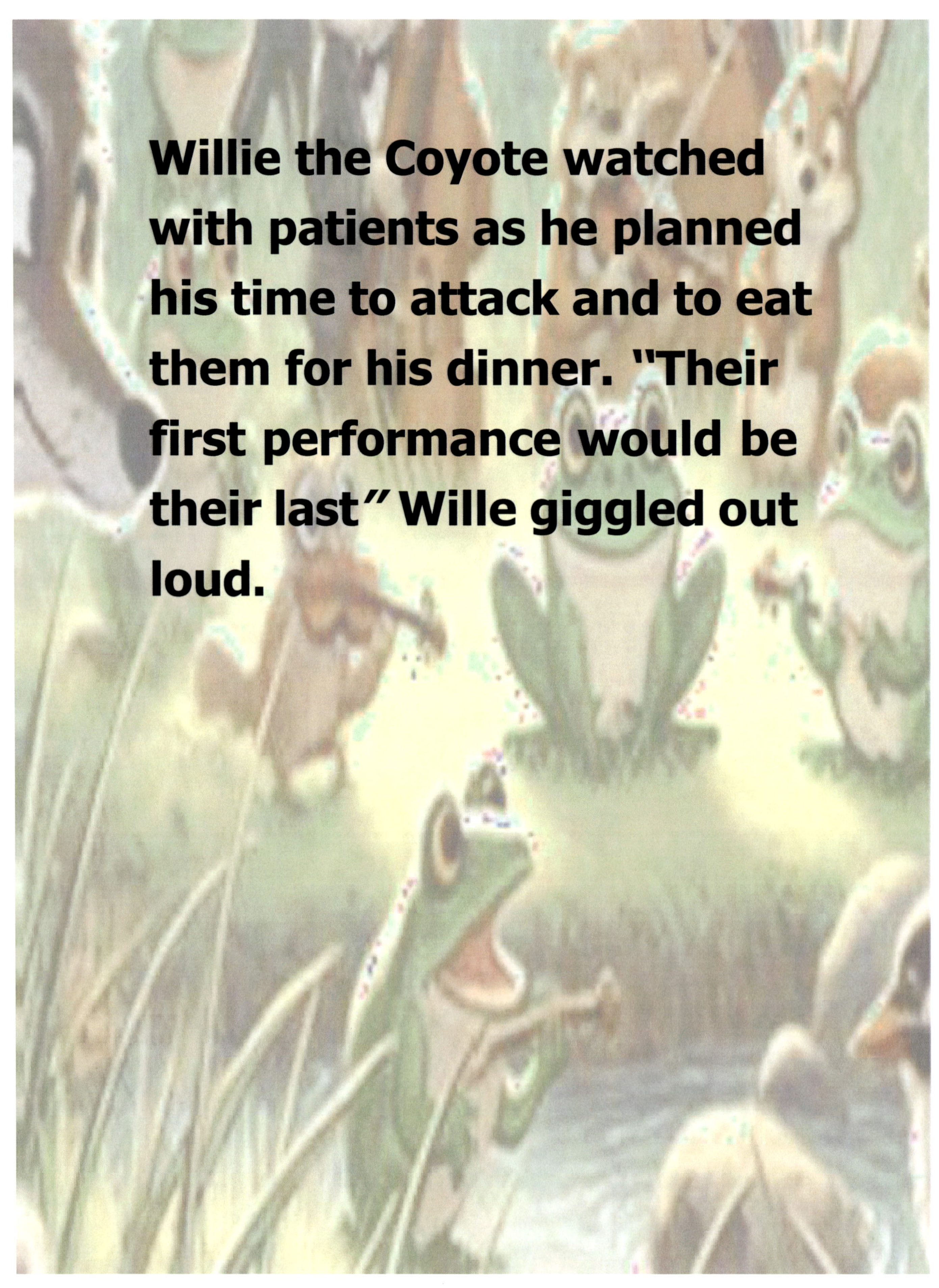
Willie the Coyote watched with patients as he planned his time to attack and to eat them for his dinner. "Their first performance would be their last" Wille giggled out loud.

WILLIE

So, he waited for his opportunity to strike. The next day they would all meet 1 hour before the start of the event to prepare for their first concert. They lined up as they took their places on stage. Willie the coyote said to himself, "How nice they are lining up for me to pounce on them all at once." Willie gets close then leaps at Dana the orchestra leader and misses.

Marvin jumps high upon a tree branch out of the reach of Willie. Willie looks for the Marvin but could not find him hiding in the tree.

Marvin points at Dana and the cricket began to play his violin music to distract the coyote from finding Marvin's hiding place.

Dana pointed at the frogs to
begin to croak with their loud
bass voices as they splashed
in the pond.   Marvin pointed
at the owl to join in with his
loud hoot, hoot, hoot

Start croaking!
Hoot!

Marvin then pointed to Rick the raccoon to make his hissing and growling noise to scare the coyote. Willie the coyote was a big coward and feared the sound was coming from a pack of wild dogs.

?!
HISS!

Marvin pointed at Arline and her friends the nightjars, who flew around Willie's head. They made a loud trilling sound that scared the coyote so bad that he tripped over a boulder onto his back into the pond.

Marvin pointed to Fred and Chris the bats to flutter around the coyote's head which made him dizzy as he tripped and fell to the ground.

Next, he pointed to Steven who was quite distressed and very annoyed by this time and as the coyote stepped out of the pond, Steven let out a loud spray right in the face of the coyote. Willie ran off into the forest yowling and screaming, and could be herd saying. "I got to get away from this place it's not safe here."

STINKY!

Finally, Evon came to the stage and made a loud scream SCREAMMM and raised he beautiful tail and everyone new that the attack was over and all was at peace.

Marvin the frog choir leader had now conducted the greatest symphony of his life and had achieved his dream of being a conductor. He had gotten a chance to conduct his greatest orchestra and make the best music that any of them had ever heard.

Later that night they put on their performance and the animals of the forest loved

Everyone had played their part just as Marvin had trained them. Who would have known that their training and working together allowed them to make an orchestra that produced beautiful music but also saved the lives of his friends.

Marvin gave thanks to his maker. Marvin also requests that all of you readers to follow your dreams. You too can be part of a wonderful symphony on day. The End

Willie finally come to his senses and realized that he was not a killer and wanted to be loved by other. So, about a week later after Steven's stinky spray had washed off of Wille the coyote turned a new leaf. He had learned his lesson and decided no more eating little animals anymore, only fish, vegetable, and fruit.

He asked Dana and Marvin to forgive him for his previous ac-tions, and they forgave him.

Later in life its said that Willie decided to learn to play the drums, and became one of the best drummers in the forest.

About the Book

The Cricket and the Frog, readers are invited into a magical tale where the harmony of the forest comes alive through the power of music and unity. Marvin, the diligent and passionate conductor, dreams of creating a symphony that captures the true essence of the forest's sounds. With unwavering dedication, he handpicks the perfect voices among the forest's inhabitants to join his choir. His search leads him to Dana, a cricket .

however, lurking in the shadows is Willie, a cunning and menacing coyote with plans far darker than mere admiration—he aims to turn the orchestra into his next meal.

The story unfolds with suspense and heart as Marvin's leadership and the animals' courage are tested in the face of danger. Readers will be captivated by how the orchestra bands together to outwit Willie and fulfill Marvin's dream.

9 781088 003411